MR.GRUMBLE

MR. GRUMBLE

by Roger Hargreaves

Mr Grumble's name suited him well!

"Bah!" he would grumble, every morning,
when his alarm clock rang.
"It's the start of yet another
horrible day!"

"Bah!" he would groan every afternoon,
on his walk in the country.
"I hate the countryside!"

One day, just after he said this,
someone suddenly appeared by magic.

It was a wizard.

A wizard, to whom Mr Grumble had the
nerve to say, "Bah! I hate wizards who
suddenly appear by magic."

"Really?" said the wizard.
"Well, I don't like people who are constantly
grumbling and moaning. I'll tell you what
I do to people who have bad manners.
I turn them into ...

... little pigs!"

And the wizard disappeared,
leaving behind him a very piggy-
looking Mr Grumble.

Mr Grumble was afraid that he might
remain a pig for the rest of his life.

But five minutes later,
by magic, of course,
he changed back into his old self.

He set off again and happened to pass
Little Miss Fun's house.

"Come in!" she cried.
"I'm having a party!"

Mr Grumble went in, but when he heard
Little Miss Fun's guests singing and
laughing he scowled.

"Bah!" he moaned.
"I can't stand singing and laughing!"

He would have done better to
have kept quiet, because ...

... the wizard appeared once more.

"I see that my first lesson
wasn't enough!" he said.
"If I'm going to teach you to stop grumbling,
groaning and moaning, I'll have to do
more than turn you into a little pig,
I'll have to turn you into ...

... a big pig!"

Mr Grumble did not like it one bit.

Little Miss Fun and her guests, however, found it very funny.

"Please," begged Mr Grumble,
"turn me back to normal!
I promise that I will never grumble,
groan or moan ever again!"

And he feebly wiggled his curly tail.

The wizard took pity on him,
and changed him back into his old self.

And then the wizard disappeared again.

Then Little Miss Fun jumped on to a table
and pretended to be a clown.

Mr grumble was not amused.

"Bah!" he snorted.
"I can't stand people who jump onto tables
and pretend to be clowns!"

You can guess what happened next.

He turned into ...

... an enormous pig!

An enormous pig whose face was
red with embarrassment!

"Oink!" wailed Mr Grumble, mournfully.

Then, this enormous red-faced pig,
made a solemn promise.

"Never again will I grumble, groan,
moan or snort!"

"Good," said the wizard,
suddenly appearing once again.

And Mr Grumble changed back
into his old self.

Well, not exactly his old self!

Look at that nice smile on his face.

Amazing, isn't it?

Later, Mr Grumble went home.

And, tired out after his exhausting day,
he went straight to bed.

He slept the whole night
without once grumbling,
groaning, moaning or snorting.

But not without ...

... snoring!

MR. MEN question time - can you help?
10 sets of 4 Mr. Men titles to be won!

Thank you for purchasing this Mr. Men book. We would be most grateful if you would help us with the answers to a few questions. Each questionnaire received will be placed in a monthly draw - you could win four Mr. Men books of your choice and a free bookmark! See overleaf.

Is this the first Mr. Men book you have purchased?   Yes ☐   No ☐ (please tick)

If No, how many books do you have in your collection?   ____

Have you collected any Little Miss books?   Yes ☐   No ☐   How many ____

Where do you usually shop for children's books?   Bookshop ☐   Supermarket ☐   Elsewhere ☐

(Can you name the retailer) _____

Which is your favourite Mr. Men character?   _____

Which is your favourite Little Miss character?   _____

Apart from Mr. Men/Little Miss which are your next two favourite children's characters?

1) _____   2) _____

Thank you for your help.
Return this form to: Marketing Department, Egmont Books Limited,
Unit 7, Millbank House, Riverside Park, Bollin Walk, Wilmslow, Cheshire SK9 1BJ.
Please tick overleaf which four Mr. Men books you would like to receive if you are successful in our monthly draw and fill in your name and address details.

Signature of parent or guardian: _____   Age of Mr. Men fan: _____

We may occasionally wish to advise you of other children's books that we publish. If you would rather we didn't, please tick this box ☐

- ☐ 1. Mr. Tickle
- ☐ 2. Mr. Greedy
- ☐ 3. Mr. Happy
- ☐ 4. Mr. Nosey
- ☐ 5. Mr. Sneeze
- ☐ 6. Mr. Bump
- ☐ 7. Mr. Snow
- ☐ 8. Mr. Messy
- ☐ 9. Mr. Topsy-Turvy
- ☐ 10. Mr. Silly
- ☐ 11. Mr. Uppity
- ☐ 12. Mr. Small
- ☐ 13. Mr. Daydream
- ☐ 14. Mr. Forgetful
- ☐ 15. Mr. Jelly
- ☐ 16. Mr. Noisy
- ☐ 17. Mr. Lazy
- ☐ 18. Mr. Funny
- ☐ 19. Mr. Mean
- ☐ 20. Mr. Chatterbox
- ☐ 21. Mr. Fussy
- ☐ 22. Mr. Bounce
- ☐ 23. Mr. Muddle
- ☐ 24. Mr. Dizzy
- ☐ 25. Mr. Impossible
- ☐ 26. Mr. Strong
- ☐ 27. Mr. Grumpy
- ☐ 28. Mr. Clumsy
- ☐ 29. Mr. Quiet
- ☐ 30. Mr. Rush
- ☐ 31. Mr. Tall
- ☐ 32. Mr. Worry
- ☐ 33. Mr. Nonsense
- ☐ 34. Mr. Wrong
- ☐ 35. Mr. Skinny
- ☐ 36. Mr. Mischief
- ☐ 37. Mr. Clever
- ☐ 38. Mr. Busy
- ☐ 39. Mr. Slow
- ☐ 40. Mr. Brave
- ☐ 41. Mr. Grumble
- ☐ 42. Mr. Perfect
- ☐ 43. Mr. Cheerful
- ☐ 44. Mr. Cool
- ☐ 45. Mr. Rude
- ☐ 46. Mr. Good

Your name _____

Address _____

_____

_____ Postcode _____